Prescott Red—
On the Farm

Mary C. A. McNamara

ISBN: Softcover   978-1-9845-0950-5
        EBook   978-1-9845-0951-2

Print information available on the last page

Rev. date: 03/08/2018

To order additional copies of this book, contact:
Xlibris
1-888-795-4274
www.Xlibris.com
Orders@Xlibris.com

Dedicated to a little red dog, with a black tail, who had a few fleas, but they're dead now – Prescott Red, and every class I have had the pleasure to teach.

Prescott Red's whelping picture with his parents: Mr. and Mrs. Dachshund,
September 9 - Prescott Farm.

Prescott Red was a little red dog, with a long body, short legs, a black tail, and a few fleas. He had shiny black toenails, which made him very handsome. He lived on Prescott Farm. The farm was way out in the country, and boasted big red tomatoes, green ones, and to Prescott's delight even a few green horned worms.

One fine morning, the warmth of the rising sun hit old Red Rooster smack in his feathery face and he crowed right outside Prescott's barn door. Prescott got up, slurped up some milk, chewed on a stick to clean his white canine teeth, brushed up against a barn pillar to straighten his smooth red coat, and off he went. "Where are you off to today?" White Cat meowed when Prescott's paws reached the farm lane. White Cat Thumper lived two barns over. She was very fond of the little red dog with a black tail, and did not mind Prescott's fleas.

"Good Morning, White Cat," Prescott happily barked. "What brings you out so early?" White Cat always seemed to know Prescott's schedule. Prescott did not mind, and with light paws in step, the two skipped down the lane careful not to step on the black darkling beetles out dancing in the morning sun.

With a green horned worm still in her mouth, a hairy legged beauty quietly crossed the lane. "There's Ula," Prescott barked to White Cat, "She's pretty nice, and fuzzy too, maybe, we can pet her!" "Good Morning, Tarantula." Prescott barked. Ula wearily stretched out one of her hairy eight legs in a good night greeting as she crawled, down, down into the earth to her silk spun home for a good day's sleep. "She's in charge of pest control," White Cat meowed in a whisper, "I don't think she likes fleas either!"

Peeps and croaks of green and yellow spotted frogs led the dual up the lane to the farm pond. Now Prescott was not fond of the duck pond, mainly because Mother Duck Quacker was not fond of him, or his fleas. She managed the pond and all the ducks in it, and it seemed it was her job not only to keep slimy snails and worms out, but Prescott out as well. Not to mention, she was still mad about the skinny dipping episode last summer. You see, it had been a very hot day and Prescott was skipping past the pond, when he skipped, tripped, and dipped! Things had not been the same since.

As the two approached the pond, White Cat hid, and Prescott got even lower to the ground than usual with his paws stepping as fast as four paws could, but the baby ducks spotted his shiny black toenails and quacked aloud in delight! They loved the little red dog with the black tail and secretly wished he would skip, trip, and dip again. An alerted mother duck waddled out of the pond and chased the little red dog up the lane quacking the whole time. "Run, Prescott," White Cat beowd, "or she'll peck you!" White "Tiger" Cat then pounced out from behind a rock, and Mother Duck dove back in the pond.

"That's Mother Duck," Prescott sighed to White Cat, "she's upset!" Then not quite looking where his paws were stepping, Prescott found himself smack in an open green pasture with a rather large creature looking down at him. "Why are you and your fleas in my pasture?" the big cow mooed smacking at one of Prescott's fleas with the whip of her tail. Prescott quickly barked out the word "milk" then the proud dairy cow strolled over to fresh bowls of it. Prescott and White Cat slurped some up; found out the cow's name, which was Mamoo; thanked her for her hospitality, and with bellies full, went on their way.

Loud bleating cries could be heard in the distance . . . "that's Oat!" Prescott barked loudly to White Cat. "He wants us to come over and play! Shall we go?" Oat was a brown and white speckled goat with floppy ears who lived with his hairy, brown speckled sister, Oata, high on a hill overlooking the farm. The two were the farm's gardeners. Every time the green grass got too high, they were invited out to eat. They could eat grass all day long, but sometimes they needed a break, and Prescott was that break! They loved to roll him back and forth like a tootsie roll on newly manicured green grass. If he rolled slow, the grass was too high, and if he rolled fast and slick, the grass was just right. Prescott liked the game and headed on over. He soon found himself rolling back and forth, back and forth, and being the great gardeners the goats were, Prescott rolled licitly split through the grass out of control down the hill past big red tomatoes, green ones, and the green horned worms, who snapped their necks just to watch him roll. He and his fleas finally landed with a thud in front of a horse pulling a cart filled with red ripe tomatoes.

Morse the horse lurked back, "Hay, Prescott! Fancy seeing you. Where did you roll in from?" "Hay, Morse. Well, I was up on the hill a minute ago." Prescott barked, scratching one of the fleas on his head. "Where you off to, Morse?" "Off to the market with the red-ripes." Morse neighed. "Climb on board, I will give you and your fleas a lift." "To the pig pen, please," Prescott barked politely, "I need a bath."

Pinkly dressed pigs squealed and oinked as they played in a wet pool of dark mud. "Come in and play, Prescott Red!" Prescott shyly put one paw in, then another, then he jumped in, "off with the fleas," he barked out, and landed right in the thick mud. The pigs rolled him once, rolled him twice, then three times until he was no longer red. The pigs then pushed him out of the mud, and laid the little brown muddy dog out in the hot sun to dry. The mud caked, then cracked, then Prescott shook it off, and with the mud went the fleas!

With no more fleas, Prescott happily headed down the lane, but soon found himself being chased by angry farm hens, "Bwak, bwak, bwak!" "I'll go get her!" Prescott barked back at the angry hens. Then he hurried off to the chicken coop only to find White Cat trying to make friends with the chickens again. White Cat looked up long enough from the chicken chase to see Prescott's raised lip and teeth, and knew the social call was over. "See you later, little peckers!" a breathless White Cat panted. Then the little red dog, with a black tail, who had a few fleas, but they're dead now, walked on home. White Cat Thumper followed.

Made in the USA
Las Vegas, NV
01 January 2022